THE ADVENTURES OF
DANIEL BOOM
A.K.A. LOUD BOY

GROW UP!

WRITTEN BY D. J. STEINBERG

ILLUSTRATED BY BRIAN SMITH

GROSSET & DUNLAP
AN IMPRINT OF PENGUIN GROUP (USA) INC.

What are our five heroes doing?
They may look like Loud
Boy, Chatterbox, Tantrum
Girl, Destructo-Kid, and
Fidget, but—a CANE?
KNITTING NEEDLES?
SHUFFLEBOARD?
THE *PRUNE GAZETTE*?!
Why in the name of Pete are they
acting like a bunch of old people?
Something is WRONG here—very, very wrong . . .

Are these the same five kids who kaboshed bad guys everywhere with their youthful powers . . . ?

DANIEL BOOM

DANIEL BOOM, who discovered his Decibel Power as LOUD BOY . . .

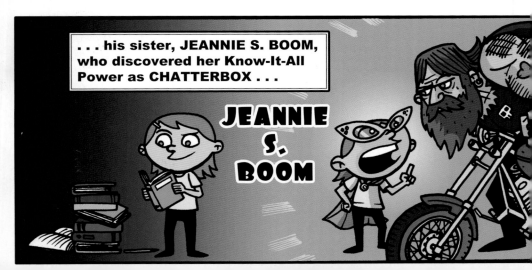

. . . his sister, JEANNIE S. BOOM, who discovered her Know-It-All Power as CHATTERBOX . . .

JEANNIE S. BOOM

REX RODRIGUEZ

. . . REX RODRIGUEZ, who found the wonders of his Chaos Power as DESTRUCTO-KID . . .

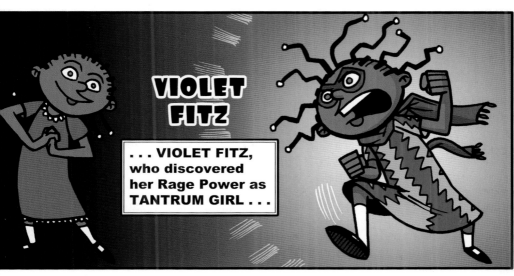

VIOLET FITZ

. . . VIOLET FITZ, who discovered her Rage Power as TANTRUM GIRL . . .

SID DOWN

. . . and SID DOWN, who discovered his unstoppable Power of Perpetual Motion as FIDGET . . .

DID I . . . ?

WAY TO ERUPT A VOLCANO, TANTRUM GIRL!

ONLY ONE ROCK MADE IT THOURGH!

YES, ONE ROCK. TWO MILLION TONS . . .

. . . WHICH, AT A VELOCITY OF 500 MILES PER HOUR, SHOULD BE FORCEFUL ENOUGH TO KNOCK THE EARTH 6.3 DEGREES OFF AXIS, SETTING OFF A SECOND ICE AGE . . .

. . . IN EXACTLY 46 SECONDS, IF MY CALCULATIONS ARE RIGHT.

HMM.

HEY, THIS TREE—CHECK IT OUT! A CLASSIC HEVEA BRASILIENSIS! YOU KNOW—A 'RUBBER TREE'!

WHAT? DON'T YOU GUYS EVER WATCH THE DENDROLOGY CHANNEL?

29 SECONDS . . .

RUBBER TREE?

STAND BACK!

☆ ABC 123

CLASS, WE HAVE A VERY SPECIAL VISITOR. MRS. BOOM?

THANK YOU, MR. STICKLER.

PSST—DANIEL—WHAT'S YOUR MOM DOING HERE?

I AM DELIGHTED TO BE THE ORGANIZER OF STILLVILLE'S FIRST EVER BRING YOUR CHILD TO WORK DAY, SPONSORED BY K. R. INDUSTRIES, WHERE MANY OF YOUR PARENTS WORK.

WE ENCOURAGE EVERY CHILD TO SIGN UP!

WHAT A TERRIFIC OPPORTUNITY!

IT'S TRUE. IN FACT, I CAN TELL YOU A STORY. WHEN MY JEANNIE S. WAS TWO, SHE DIDN'T SPEAK **AT ALL.** THEN ONE DAY SHE VISITED MY OLD OFFICE IN NEW GRIDLOCK AND WAS SO STIMULATED THAT RIGHT THEN AND THERE, SHE STARTED SPEAKING IN **FULL PARAGRAPHS!**

. . . . HA HA . . . AND SHE HASN'T STOPPED SINCE!

WHY DOES MOM ALWAYS HAVE TO TELL EVERYONE OUR FAMILY STORIES?

BUT, EXCUSE ME, MRS. BOOM. WHAT IF WE DON'T WANT TO GO?

BUT WHY, VIOLET?

LIKE, LET'S SAY, FOR INSTANCE, YOU KNEW THAT YOUR PARENTS WORKED FOR A TOTALLY EVIL CORPORATION?

HA HA HA —evil . . .

IT'S NOT FUNNY. I'M SERIOUS. EVERYBODY KNOWS K.R. INDUSTRIES IS EVIL . . .

Ooo—eeeeevil!

THAT IS NOT TRUE! THAT IS A BUNCH OF COMPLETE AND UTTER MALARKEY!

IT IS TRUE, MOM! JEANNIE S. AND I HAVE BEEN TRYING TO TELL YOU, BUT YOU NEVER BELIEVE US.

booga, booga, booga!

I AM SICK AND TIRED OF YOU KIDS MAKING UP TALL TALES! K.R. INDUSTRIES IS A GOOD COMPANY THAT MAKES GOOD THINGS FOR PEOPLE.

BUT, MRS. BOOM . . .

. . . DON'T YOU KNOW K.R. STANDS FOR KID-RID?

THAT IS ABSURD!

AND IT'S RUN BY MEAN, OLD SCIENTISTS!

CLASS . . . CLASS . . .

QUIET!

OOGA, BOOGA, BOOGA!

WOULD YOU STOP IT!

HA HA HA

VIOLET FITZ, THAT MEANS YOU!

BUT, MR. STICKLER, HE WAS MAKING FACES AT ME.

THEN IGNORE HIM.

I CAN'T.

YES, YOU CAN.

SERIOUSLY—IT'S SCIENTIFIC. WHEN YOU'RE A KID AND SOMEBODY MAKES A FACE AT YOU, YOU FREAK OUT. YOU CAN'T HELP IT— IT'S KIND OF A LAW OF BEING A KID.

THAT'S TRUE, MR. STICKLER.

IT'S SCIENTIFIC.

WELL THEN, I AM TELLING YOU ALL RIGHT NOW—AND THIS IS SCIENTIFIC: YOU'D BETTER **GROW UP** IF YOU DON'T WANT TO FIND YOURSELF IN PRINCIPAL MINTZ'S OFFICE!

WRAAAAAAARGH!

SMASH!

VIOLET, THIS IS YOUR 43RD TIME IN MY OFFICE. DR. AHA AND I BELIEVE IT'S TIME TO TALK WITH YOUR PARENTS ABOUT A . . .

PRINCIPAL MINTZ

. . . LOVELY ROOM-AND-BOARD FACILITY IN PINKERTON THAT SPECIALIZES IN THESE SORTS OF . . . ER, ISSUES.

PRINCIPAL MINTZ

NO! PRINCIPAL MINTZ—PLEASE. MY FRIENDS ARE ALL HERE AT STILLVILLE ELEMENTARY. I DON'T WANT TO LEAVE. PLEASE. DON'T SEND ME TO PINKERTON.

PINKERTON HAS A BEAUTIFUL, PEACEFUL CAMPUS—I KNOW YOU WILL LOVE IT THERE!

WHAT'S GOING ON?

THEY'RE GOING TO SEND HER TO PINKERTON!

NO!

BUT . . . BUT . . . I PROMISE, I'LL DO ANYTHING. PLEEEASE. I'LL BE REALLY, REALLY BETTER.

PSST PSST PSST . . .

WELL, OUR SCHOOL PSYCHOLOGIST IS WILLING TO ADMINISTER AN ANGER MANAGEMENT TEST AT 3:00 P.M. NEXT FRIDAY.

IF YOU CAN PASS AND DEMONSTRATE FULL SELF-RESTRAINT, WE CAN ALLOW YOU TO STAY . . .

. . . BUT IF YOU DO NOT, VIOLET FITZ, YOU UNDERSTAND— WE WILL HAVE NO OTHER CHOICE.

I SAID— AGH!

DID HE SAY 'AGH'?

UNCLE STANLEY, DID YOU SAY 'AGH'?

HELLO, CHILDREN. THIS IS UNCLE STANLEY.

I WAS SAYING THAT YOU MUST ALL PROMISE TO COME TO K. R. NEXT FRIDAY FOR THE BRING YOUR CHILD TO WORK DAY.

SURE, BUT . . . UNCLE STANLEY? YOU SOUND KIND OF FUNNY.

YES, I JUST HAVE A LITTLE . . . AHEM . . . COLD.

I'LL SEE YOU—COUGH, COUGH—LATER, CHILDREN.

OKAY, WELL, FEEL BETTER, UNCLE STANLEY.

UNCLE STANLEY'S RIGHT! THIS EVENT IS THE PERFECT OPPORTUNITY TO SPY FROM THE INSIDE! ONCE WE'RE IN THE K.R. OFFICES, JUST THINK OF THE POSSIBILITIES . . .

GUYS, CAN YOU KEEP IT DOWN? I ONLY HAVE A WEEK TO STUDY FOR MY TANTRUM TEST.

OH. SORRY, VIOLET.

COME ON, GUYS. LET'S LET VIOLET STUDY.

FINDING YOUR HAPPY PLACE

BREATHE IN, BREATHE OUT . . .

RELAXATION 1·2·3

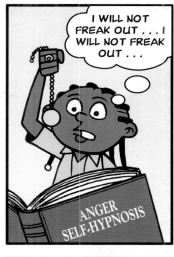

I WILL NOT FREAK OUT . . . I WILL NOT FREAK OUT . . .

ANGER SELF·HYPNOSIS

OHMMM . . .

MEDITATION FOR DUMMIES

DANCE AWAY YOUR DEMONS

TEMPER TANTRUM HOMEOPATHY

SELF·ACUPUNCTURE

BOOF!

KICKBOX YOUR STRESS AWAY!

EAT YOUR STRESS AWAY!

YOU MADE IT, VIOLET!

ONE WEEK TANTRUM-FREE.

I KNOW. THOSE BOOKS REALLY WORK!

YOU'RE GOING TO ACE THAT TEST TOMORROW— I KNOW IT.

TO VIOLET!

. . . THANKS, YOU GUYS. I COULDN'T HAVE DONE IT WITHOUT—

HUH?

FOOEY, I GOT TEA ON MY SWEATER.

I HATE IT WHEN I GET TEA ON MY SWEATER. THIS IS MY FAVORITE NEW SWEATER! AND IT'S A POLYESTER, DRY-CLEAN ONLY BLEND!!

WHOOPSIES.

IT'S OKAY. NO BIGGY.

JUST A LITTLE SLIP. DOESN'T MEAN ANYTHING.

WHO AM I KIDDING? I'M DOOMED. I'VE BEEN CRAMMING FOR A WEEK, MY TANTRUM TEST IS AT THREE O'CLOCK TOMORROW, AND I'M HEADED TO PINKERTON!

THAT'S IT. I HAVE TO STAY HOME AND STUDY TOMORROW.

NO—YOU HAVE TO GO TO K.R. FOR THE BRING YOUR CHILD EVENT. UNCLE STANLEY SAID WE ALL HAVE TO BE THERE. WE PROMISED, REMEMBER?

I CAN'T.

YES, YOU CAN. JUST BRING YOUR NOTES ALONG TO THE FIELD TRIP. WE'LL BLOCK FOR YOU AND MAKE SURE YOU CAN STUDY.

REALLY? THINK THAT'LL WORK?

SURE THING!

YOU BET!

Next morning . . .

WELCOME, CHILDREN, TO THE WORLD-WIDE HEADQUARTERS OF K. R. INDUSTRIES FOR OUR FIRST EVER **BRING YOUR CHILD TO WORK DAY.**

K. R. INDUSTRIES

FOR INSTANCE, K.R.'S EXTRA-STICKY FORMULA, SUPER-STICK DENTURE GLUE . . .

. . . OR WHO CAN FORGET K.R.'S AWARD-WINNING AGE-SPOT ZAPPER SAP . . .

. . . OR THE MIRACULOUS ABSORBENCY BREAK-THROUGH OF THIS XXL ADULT DIAPER . . .

MRS. BOOM, HOW COME EVERYTHING AT K.R. IS OLD PEOPLE STUFF?

OH, NOW—IT'S NOT ALL OLD PEOPLE STUFF. I MEAN, WE ALSO HAVE . . .

NEW AND IMPROVED! HEAD-SHINER FOR A BEAUTIFUL BALD!

. . . WELL, OKAY. YES—I GUESS IT'S MOSTLY ALL OLD PEOPLE STUFF, BUT . . .

. . . AND ON YOUR LEFT IS AN AREA THAT IS OFF-LIMITS TO K.R. EMPLOYEES, EXCEPT BY SPECIAL PERMISSION. YOU SEE LAB A IS WHERE THE NEWEST MOST CUTTING-EDGE IDEAS ARE TESTED OUT.

LAB A
TOP SECRET

SHE'S COMPLETELY DISAPPEARED.

WHAT DO WE DO?

WHAT DO WE DO ABOUT WHAT?

VIOLET!

THERE YOU ARE!

YOU HAD US FREAKED OUT.

OH, DON'T WORRY ABOUT ME, DEARIES.

DEARIES?

AND NOW, BOYS AND GIRLS, WE WILL HAVE A ONE-HOUR BREAK FOR LUNCH HERE AT K.R. PLAZA . . .

K.R. DOGS

K.R. ON A CONE

K.R. PIZZA

. . . WHERE YOU ARE WELCOME TO EAT AT OUR CAFETERIA AND BROWSE OUR EMPLOYEE STORES.

WOW, CHECK IT OUT, VIOLET. THIS PLACE IS LIKE A MALL.

. . . THEN, AFTER LUNCH, YOU WILL BE JOINING YOUR K.R. PARENT TO SPEND THE AFTERNOON WITH HIM OR HER.

VIOLET?

WHERE DID YOU GO NOW?

. . WELL, THANK YOU, EVERYONE, AND ENJOY THE REST OF YOUR DAY AT K.R. INDUSTRIES!

OH NO.

NOT AGAIN!

VIOLET!

IT WAS JUST TOO DARLING TO PASS UP, DON'T YOU THINK?

VIOLET, YOU BOUGHT A . . . GRANNY BAG?

AND IT WAS ON SALE, TOO!

UH, STAY RIGHT HERE, OKAY?

UNCLE STANLEY?

UNCLE STANLEY, ARE YOU THERE?

ER, YES. THIS IS UNCLE STANLEY.

IT'S ABOUT VIOLET. SHE SEEMS, WELL, A LITTLE... DIFFERENT.

I SEE... YES, WELL, SOMETIMES A COMPANY AS IMPRESSIVE AS K.R. CAN HAVE AN INITIAL OVERWHELMING EFFECT ON PEOPLE...

...BUT I'M SURE YOUR FRIEND WILL BE JUST FINE.

NOW GO ENJOY YOURSELVES. TOODLE-LOO.

TOODLE-LOO? SINCE WHEN DOES UNCLE STANLEY SAY, 'TOODLE-LOO'?

OKAY, WHO'S HUNGRY? COME ON, YOU FIVE, DIG IN.

THANKS, MOM.

THANKS, MOM.

THANKS, MRS. BOOM.

REALLY, THIS SUPERHERO FABRIC DOESN'T BREATHE . . .

VIOLET, ER, TANTRUM GIRL—COME WITH ME SO YOU DON'T DISAPPEAR ANYMORE, OKAY?

OKAY, SWEETHEART, BUT NOT TOO FAST.

DESTRUCTO-RELEASIFICATION STATION

K.R.—ELIMINATING DESTRUCTIVITY SINCE 1981

WEIRD . . . SEEMS ODDLY JUST RIGHT FOR ME.

DESTRUCTO-RELEASIFICATION STATION
K.R.—ELIMINATING DESTRUCTIVITY SINCE 1981

COME IN, REX.

DESTRUCTO-RELEASIFICATION STATION
K.R.—ELIMINATING DESTRUCTIVITY SINCE 1981

FLASHH!!

YOU GUYS OKAY?

MY FEET...

MY HEAD...

MY GLUTEUS MAXIMUS...

WE'VE GOT TO DO SOMETHING WITH THEM.

THAT'S IT. NAP TIME IN THE RESEARCH ROOM.

RESEARCH ROOM

ZZZZZ
ZZZZZ
ZZZZZ

PLEASANT RESEARCH . . . BE BACK SOON.

K.R. CENTRAL MAINFRAME
KEEP OUT

I HAVE AN IDEA. COVER ME, I'M GOING IN.

COME ON, LITTLE LOCK . . .

CLICK CLICK

H_2SO_4

SULPHURIC ACID. THAT SHOULD DO IT.

SNORF! ZZZZZZZZZZZZ... DROOL-SLURP... SNORP-SNORE! ZZZZZ BURP-WHISTLE ZZZZZZZZZZ FLEM-SCHPLIPFF! ZIZZZLE-ZAZZZLE SNORT-ZZZZZZZZ...

RESEARCH ROOM

ZZZZZ... GO, LITTLE SHUFFLEBOARD PUCK... ZZZZZZ

BE A DEAR AND CUT MY BANANAS FOR ME... WHY THANK YOU, DEARIE...

ZZZZZ... LOOK, AT LAST—THE MAGICAL FOREST OF PRUNES!

GOT IT.

AND ONE MORE THING I HAVE TO DO WHILE I'M HERE...

KR–546   KR–551

KR–547 CLICK   KR–552

KR–548   KR–553

KR–549   KR–554

KR–550   KR–55

FINALLY, I'M GOING TO FIND OUT!

TOP SECRET
EXPERIMENT FILE
KR-547 "THE ENERGY
REPLENERATOR"

NEW GRIDLOCK
BRANCH LABORATORY

-FAILURE-
PLAY ARCHIVE VIDEO

CLICK

THANK YOU, DEAR JOURNALISTS, FOR COMING TO WITNESS THIS MOMENTOUS OCCASION. EXPERIMENT KR-547, OR AS WE LIKE TO CALL IT, 'THE ENERGY REPLENERATOR,' WILL CHANGE THE WORLD AS WE KNOW IT . . .

TODAY, K.R. INDUSTRIES IS PROUD TO UNVEIL AN ALTERNATE SOURCE OF ENERGY. NO LONGER WILL THIS PLANET HAVE TO RELY ON OIL FOR ENERGY.

THIS NEW SOURCE IS A COMMODITY THAT CAN BE QUICKLY REPLENISHED. IT WILL LEAVE NO AIR POLLUTION, CARBON EMISSIONS, OR GREENHOUSE GASES— EXCEPT FOR SOME, ER, INSIGNIFICANT METHANE BI-PRODUCTS.

YES, LADIES AND GENTLEMEN OF THE PRESS, I'M TALKING ABOUT . . .

I DON'T GET IT. WHY WOULD UNCLE STANLEY THINK THAT DUMB FAILED EXPERIMENT WOULD HAVE ANYTHING TO DO WITH ME?

HE MUST HAVE MIXED UP THE NUMBER OR SOMETHING.

FAILURE

WAIT. UNLESS . . .

I WONDER . . . IF I GO BACK—THERE, TO THAT PART . . .

THERE . . . THAT FLASH FRAME.

IF I BRING DOWN THE LUMINOSITY . . .

GOOD THING I READ THAT BOOK ABOUT DIGITAL IMAGE CALIBRATION THAT TIME I WAS WAITING FOR THE BUS.

. . . ADD A GAMMA FILTER . . .

HEY, THAT'S ME!

SO THAT'S IT! THAT DAY MOM ALWAYS TALKS ABOUT WHEN SHE TOOK ME TO THE OFFICE . . .

HOLY COW, UNCLE STANLEY WAS RIGHT! THAT ENERGY BEAM . . . MY MOUTH . . . THAT EXPLAINS EVERYTHING!

KR-547 WASN'T A FAILURE AT ALL!

Back in the lab . . .

I KNOW THOSE SHOES. IT'S UNCLE STANLEY!

NUMBER 23, YOU JUST GASP?

NO, NUMBER 52, HOW 'BOUT YOU?

WELL, IF YOU DIDN'T GASP AND I DIDN'T GASP, THEN GUESS WHO MUST HAVE . . .

THANK YOU, MY FINE GOONS. IF YOU WILL PLEASE HELP OUR LAST FRIEND TO HIS SEAT . . .

YOU SEE, WE SAVED A CHAIR FOR YOU.

WHAT ARE YOU ALL DOING HERE?

SPEAK UP—DIDN'T QUITE CATCH THAT, SONNY.

NO! NOT YOU, TOO!

THAT NAUGHTY, NAUGHTY GOON MAN . . .

. . . WOKE US FROM OUR NAP . . . VERY RUDE.

OH . . . MY BACK . . .

QUIET! I WAS JUST EXPLAINING THAT A CERTAIN EXPERIMENT, KR-547, WAS DISMISSED AS A FAILURE MANY YEARS AGO, DUE TO A LITTLE 'PEST CONTROL' PROBLEM AT OUR NEW GRIDLOCK FACILITY.

BUT I THINK EVERY GREAT EXPERIMENT DESERVES A 'TAKE 2,' DON'T YOU?

FLASH!!

FLOOSHH!!!

ALBERT, IF YOU WOULD?

VVVROOOM!

IT WORKED, DOCTOR DOCTER. THE RABBIT ENERGY STARTED UP MY CAR.

FOGEY

THANK YOU, YOU ARE ALL TOO KIND.

CLAP-CLAP-CLAP

BEING THE SENTIMENTAL FELLOW I AM, I THOUGHT IT ONLY RIGHT TO HAVE MY OLD PROTÉGÉ, STANLEY BOOM, HERE TO WITNESS THIS HISTORIC MOMENT. AFTER ALL, IT WAS HIS RESEARCH THAT MADE THIS POSSIBLE IN THE FIRST PLACE.

WHAT DO YOU THINK, STANLEY?

WHOOPS, FORGOT HOW HARD IT MUST BE FOR YOU TO ANSWER WITH THAT, ER, GAG ON.

OKAY, GOONS, DISPOSE OF HIM NOW. I'LL BE HAPPY NEVER TO SEE THAT TRAITOROUS WEASEL AGAIN.

NO! LEAVE UNCLE STANLEY ALONE!

SIT DOWN, BOY. IT'S ALMOST YOUR TURN. SEE, I ALWAYS KNEW THAT THIS ENERGY REPLENERATOR COULD DO MUCH MORE THAN MERELY CONVERT RABBIT ENERGY.

SURE ENOUGH, IT SEEMS TO WORK QUITE HANDILY ON CHILDREN, GOOD FOR SUCKING UP ALL THAT WASTED **YOUTH ENERGY** . . .

. . . AS YOU CAN SEE PLAINLY FROM THESE FOUR TEST CASES RIGHT HERE IN THE ROOM.

DO I KNOW YOU, DEARIE?

OH . . . MY GALL BLADDER . . .

GOTTA GO TO THE BATHROOM.

NOW JUST ONE LAST TARGET AND I WILL HAVE ALL THE ENERGY I NEED FROM YOU FIVE MEDDLING BRATS.

NO, PLEASE!

FLASHH!!

VHOA, OOF . . .

HUH? MY VOICE. SO WEAK. IT'S—IT'S ALMOST NORMAL!

NO YOUTH ENERGY.

ANYBODY GOT A BATHROOM?

. . . NO POWERS.

FLUMP!

WITH ALL THE ENERGY SUPPLIED BY YOU HYPERACTIVE FREAKS, I NOW HAVE ENOUGH IN MY ENERGY REPLENERATOR TO REVITALIZE EVERY MEMBER OF KID-RID AROUND THE WORLD . . .

. . . STARTING WITH ME AND MY BOARD MEMBERS!

FLOOSHH!!

YES, DEARIE. UNEXPECTED, BUT . . . REFRESHING.

AHA . . .

OH . . .

AHA . . .

-RUSTLE-RUSTLE-RUSTLE-

IT'S OUTRAGEOUS . . . DISGUSTING. COME ON, KIDS, LET'S GO STOP THOSE OVERAGED BULLIES!

KIDS?

KIDS?

KNIT ONE . . . PEARL TWO . . .

I ♥ PRUNES.

STILLVILLE SENIOR CENTER

SENIOR CENTER

FIBER POWDER
New Fish Flavor!

GO, LITTLE PUCK!

TIME FOR YOUR FIBER, CHATTERBOX.

WHAT? SPEAK UP, SONNY BOY.

WHAT EXACTLY DO YOU KIDS THINK YOU ARE DOING?!

UNCLE STANLEY, IT'S JUST SO . . . PEACEFUL HERE.

NOT TO MENTION SERENE.

AND LOOK, THEY HAVE BINGO HERE!

GUYS, YOU'RE TOO YOUNG FOR THIS PLACE! BEING OLD IS GREAT FOR OLD PEOPLE, BUT BEING YOUNG AIN'T SO BAD.

DON'T YOU WANT TO BE ABLE TO RUN WHEN YOU WANT TO RUN, SHOUT WHEN YOU WANT TO SHOUT, SAVE THE WORLD WHEN YOU WANT TO SAVE THE WORLD?

COULDN'T QUITE HEAR HIM, BUT I THINK HE HAS A POINT.

TRUE. RETIREMENT ISN'T ALL IT'S CRACKED UP TO BE.

JUST A LITTLE ENERGY WOULD BE NICE.

I GOTTA GO TO THE BATHROOM.

YOU JUST WENT!

EXCUSE ME, I'M AFRAID I AM GOING TO HAVE TO ASK YOU TO LEAVE.

DID HE SAY HE WAS 'AFRAID'?

I'M THINKING THAT'S WHAT HE SAID.

HE PROBABLY SHOULD BE AFRAID.

I'M AFRAID WE'RE GOING TO HAVE TO ASK **YOU** TO LEAVE, SIR.

CRASH!

OOOOWWWW!

AAAAAAAAAH!

DON'T TELL ME. A BUNCH OF CRANKY, OLD BULLIES?

UH-HUH. LED BY SOME WACKO DOCTOR!

WE'RE HERE TO STOP THEM.

H-HOW?

GOOD QUESTION . . .

THEY'RE UNSTOPPABLE. INCORRIGIBLE. THEY—THEY'RE ACTING LIKE A BUNCH OF KIDS!

BINGO! THAT'S IT! I GOT IT.

HA HA HA . . .

WHAT'S SO FUNNY, OLD MAN?

YOU!

YOU THINKING THAT YOU CAN BEAT US, JUST BECAUSE WE'RE OLD. WELL, THE WORLD'S ABOUT TO CHANGE, AMIGO!

STOP!

HUH? SAYS WHO?

YOU READY, DEARIES?

. . . GO!

EW. HE'S MAKING FACES AT ME.

YIKES!

HEY! WHAT ARE YOU DOING? STOP THAT!

HEY, CUT THAT OUT!

WHY ARE THEY DOING THAT? THEY'RE FREAKING ME OUT!

TOLD YOU—IT'S SCIENTIFIC. IT ALWAYS WORKS ON KIDS.

STOP IT. ENOUGH! ALL RIGHT ALREADY . . . WHAT WILL IT TAKE TO MAKE YOU KIDS STOP?

COME HERE, AND I'LL TELL YOU.

TELL ME, BOY. I DON'T HAVE ALL DAY.

THANKS.

GIMME THAT, YOU TWERP.

UNCLE STANLEY, DO YOU KNOW HOW IT WORKS?

DO I KNOW? I INVENTED IT!

AND THEN IF I PRESS OVER HERE . . .

FLOOSHH!!

WE'RE BACK!

I FEEL LIKE A KID AGAIN.

MY HAIR! EEKS! WHAT DID I DO?!

UM, KIDS, THEY'RE GETTING AWAY!

YOU KNOW WHAT I'VE BEEN JUST DYING TO DO?

WHAT'S THAT, LOUD BOY?

OFFICER, I THOUGHT YOU MIGHT FIND THIS INTERESTING. THIS CD CONTAINS A COMPLETE RECORD OF KID-RID'S CONSPIRACY AGAINST CHILDREN, RIPPED FROM THE TOP SECRET MAINFRAME AT K.R. INDUSTRIES, A CORPORATION WHICH HAS BEEN A FRONT FOR THIS GROUP OF EVILDOERS SINCE ITS INCEPTION IN 1981. NOT THAT THERE AREN'T PLENTY OF GOOD PEOPLE WHO WORK AT K.R. . . . LIKE MY MOM, FOR INSTANCE . . .

OH.

SPEAKING OF MOM. . .

KIDS?

MOM?

AFTER LAST WEEK'S SCANDAL, IN WHICH THE C.E.O. AND ENTIRE BOARD OF DIRECTORS OF THE POWERHOUSE K.R. INDUSTRIES WERE ARRESTED ON CHARGES OF BULLYING . . .

. . . A PETITION FROM THE COMPANY'S EMPLOYEES HAS BEEN RATIFIED FOR K.R., TO BE RUN BY ONE OF ITS FIRST EMPLOYEES, WHO HAS RESURFACED AFTER A DECADE-LONG DISAPPEARANCE.

I AM REFERRING TO MR. STANLEY BOOM.

STANLEY. FIRST OFF, WHERE HAVE YOU BEEN THESE LAST TEN YEARS?

OH . . . HERE, THERE. YOU KNOW THE LIFE OF A TRAVELING INVENTOR.

AND HOW DOES IT FEEL TO BE GOING BACK TO K.R.?

I'VE ALWAYS KNOWN WHAT THIS COMPANY COULD DO. NOW, MY COMMITTEE AND I CAN STEER ITS WORK TO TRULY MAKE THE WORLD A BETTER PLACE. LIKE AN IDEA WE HAVE FOR A CEREAL BOWL THAT REGULATES THE CEREAL-TO-MILK RATIO TO ENSURE YOU NEVER RUN OUT OF CEREAL BEFORE MILK OR MILK BEFORE YOUR CEREAL . . .

I'M SORRY. YOU SAID—YOUR 'COMMITTEE'?

YES, FIVE OF MY MOST TRUSTED FRIENDS, WHO HAVE CONVINCED ME TO HOLD OUR BOARD MEETINGS IN A TREE HOUSE. EXACTLY THE KIND OF THINKING THAT WILL REENERGIZE K.R.

I SEE. ONE LAST QUESTION: CAN YOU ANSWER A LONG HELD MYSTERY— WHAT DOES THE 'K.R.' STAND FOR?

I AM QUITE POSITIVE IT STANDS FOR 'KIDS RULE.'

WELL, THANKS FOR JOINING US. ONCE AGAIN, OUR GUEST WAS STANLEY BOOM . . .

YOU WERE GREAT, UNCLE STANLEY!

YOU'RE GOING TO BE THE BEST BOSS EVER IN THE HISTORY OF BOSSES.

THINK YOU'LL INSTALL CANDY MACHINES IN THE LOBBY? LIKE THE KIND WITH THE FAMILY-SIZE BARS?

WILL YOU PUT A SKATEBOARD LANE IN ALL THE HALLWAYS?

OF COURSE! ANYTHING YOU KIDS WANT. AFTER ALL, I COULD NEVER HAVE DONE IT WITHOUT YOU.

OH NO, GUYS— WE'RE LATE FOR SCHOOL AGAIN!

COME ON, WE'LL TAKE THE ROCKET. I CAN DROP YOU ALL OFF ON MY WAY TO THE OFFICE!

And that, dear friends, is how Doctor Docter and his evil corporation were undone and a new day was born for our five friends and the man they called "uncle." But what, you may ask, happened to the legions of Kid-Rid followers all over the world? Can a force of evil that deep and dark truly be vanquished? Perhaps we both know the answer. But perhaps we also know that, whatever may come, no force in the world can be greater than that of pure and unapologetic youth.

THE END . . .*

* PERHAPS?